My Princess Collection

Aurora

A Dream Come True

Book Nine

Adapted from *Princess Aurora: Once Upon a Dream*,
written by Grace Windsor
For information address Disney Press, 114 Fifth Avenue,
New York, New York 10011-5690.
First Edition
Printed in China
9 10 8
ISBN 0-7868-4602-X

For more Disney Press fun,
visit www.disneybooks.com

Chapter One

I'm Princess Aurora, and I'm married to Prince Phillip. But it seems like only yesterday that Prince Phillip rescued me from the evil fairy, Maleficent.

It all began on the day I was born. My father, King Stefan, had invited many guests to celebrate my birth, including the fairies Flora, Fauna, and Merryweather.

Flora gave me the gift of beauty. "Lips that shame the red, red rose," she said with a wave of her wand.

Fauna conjured a flock of birds and gave me the gift of song.

But before Merryweather could give me her gift, the evil fairy Maleficent entered the room with a terrible burst of flames.

Maleficent was angry because no one had invited her to the celebration. She pointed at me and said, "Before the sun sets on her sixteenth birthday, she shall prick her finger on the spindle of a spinning wheel and die!"

The guards rushed in to capture her. But the spell had already been cast, and Maleficent had disappeared in a ball of flame!

Chapter Two

Luckily, Merryweather still hadn't given me her gift. She couldn't undo Maleficent's curse, but she could change it. And she did. So, on my sixteenth birthday, I would still prick my finger on a spinning wheel. But instead of dying, I would fall into a deep sleep. And only a kiss—True Love's Kiss—could wake me.

To protect me from Maleficent, my parents sent me away. Dressed as peasants, the three fairies took me into the forest where we would all live until I turned sixteen.

Then my father ordered that every spinning wheel in the kingdom be destroyed.

Growing up in a forest cottage, I didn't know I was a princess or that my guardians were fairies. I called them my aunties. They called me Briar Rose.

Though we were very happy, my aunties worried about me a lot. They knew that Maleficent's spies were looking for me. They warned me never to talk to strangers.

I didn't know about the curse, and I never saw anyone in the forest until one very special day. . . .

Chapter Three

It was my sixteenth birthday, and my aunties sent me out to pick berries. I had a feeling that they were planning something— a birthday party, perhaps?

I sang a song as I wandered through the woods. It was about a handsome prince I once had a dream about. In the dream, we fell in love.

Suddenly, my animal friends appeared, dressed in a cloak and boots! They pretended to be a prince and asked me to dance.

I laughed and danced with the pretend prince. When I turned around, I saw a stranger—a very handsome stranger. The stranger was exactly like the prince in my dreams! He joined me in the song, and we danced together.

When we finished singing, the handsome man asked me my name. I didn't tell him, but I invited him to our cottage for dinner. I was falling hopelessly in love with him.

Chapter Four

I returned home and told my aunties all about the handsome man. Instead of being happy for me, my aunties were upset. All in a rush, they told me the truth about who I really was. I was shocked and so happy to learn I was . . . a princess! They told me my real name was Princess Aurora.

And there was more. When I was born, my father had promised King Hubert that I would marry his son when I turned sixteen. Since that very day was my sixteenth birthday, we had to return to the castle, so I could marry a prince that I didn't even know.

I was very sad. I thought about the handsome stranger I had met that day. What would he think when he arrived for dinner to find our cottage empty? I wished I could see him again—just to say good-bye.

Although I was sad, I couldn't wait to meet my parents. For sixteen years, I hadn't even known that my parents were the King and Queen!

When we arrived at the castle, I was taken upstairs to my room. I sat thinking about my marriage. I didn't want to marry the prince—I didn't even know him. But my parents had made a promise. I would do it for them.

Chapter Five

As I sat at my dressing table, I noticed a strange green light in the fireplace. In a trance, I followed it through the castle, up a staircase to a dark room. There was an old spinning wheel in the room—the only one in the kingdom that had survived.

"Touch the spindle!" a voice called. "Touch it, I say!"

I heard my aunties calling me, and I wanted to run to them. But I couldn't. I had to obey the voice. I reached out ever so slowly and touched the spindle.

The last thing I remember is a great green fire that burst out from the spinning wheel. The fire was colder than ice! I wanted to call for help. But I couldn't. I was dizzy, and I couldn't see! I heard voices calling from far away, but before I knew it, I fell into a deep sleep.

Chapter Six

All of a sudden, I woke up to a gentle kiss. I was lying on a bed, and the stranger I had met in the forest was at my side!

"I'm Prince Phillip, King Hubert's son," he said.

"But I thought you were . . ." I began.

". . . the one who's supposed to marry you," he finished.

Prince Phillip and the man I met in the forest were the same person! It was a dream come true!

Phillip then explained that Maleficent had hypnotized me into pricking my finger on the spinning wheel. Then she kidnapped the prince as he waited for me at the cottage.

While the kingdom slept under the good fairies' protective spell, Maleficent had turned herself into a dragon! Phillip battled her with a magical sword and shield.

When Phillip and the fairies had defeated Maleficent, he kissed me. True Love's Kiss broke Maleficent's curse, and I awoke— along with every- one else in the kingdom.

Prince Phillip and I were married. Hundreds of people attended our wedding, and everyone toasted us—the royal couple!